LITTLE GROOT, BIG FEELINGS

By Kiara Valdez
Illustrated by Wendy Tan

Scholastic Inc.

ISBN 978-1-338-89032-7
10 9 8 7 6 5 4 3 2 1   23 24 25 26 27
Printed in the U.S.A.   40
First printing 2023

Book design by Martha Maynard

Usually, he has no problem playing with the big guys.

But sometimes things don't go his way.

I AM GROOOO

Groot wants to show his friends how great his room looks now.

I am Groot?

Where is everyone?
Groot is worried.

Groot starts looking for his friends.

Oh no! His friends are in trouble!

Even Groot gets scared sometimes.

But this time, he will have to be brave and save his friends.

Feelings can be strange and hard to figure out.

But friends can help you understand your feelings. Groot knows exactly what the other plant needs to feel better.

Sometimes you just need someone to cheer you on.

And friends who accept you—
no matter what.

The Children's Beading Book

INTERSTELLAR

TRADING & PUBLISHING COMPANY

LA MESA, CALIFORNIA

ISBN 0-9645957-6-1
LIBRARY OF CONGRESS CATALOG NUMBER: 96-94612
SAN: 298-5829

All illustrations by Wendy Simpson Conner
Color Photography by Don Brandos
Printed in the United States of America

FIRST PRINTING: DECEMBER, 1997

ACKNOWLEDGMENTS:
To Jennie, Priscilla, Joni and Paul;
and everyone who bought and loved
THE BEST LITTLE BEADING BOOK,
THE BEADED LAMPSHADE BOOK,
THE MAGICAL BEADED MEDICINE BAG BOOK.
THE 'KNOTTY' MACRAME AND BEADING BOOK
THE BEADED WATCHBAND BOOK
THE CHAIN & CRYSTAL BOOK
&
THE BEADED JEWELRY FOR A WEDDING BOOK

I was named for the Wendy in Peter Pan. They tell me that I would sing that "I won't grow up" song for hours on end when I was very young. Even as I get older, I still try to retain something of who I was as a child. I think it's important for all of us to retain that magic that usually stays with childhood, and gets left behind as we grow older.

I've always loved good illustration. I was exposed to the work of Arthur Rackham, Edmund Dulac, and Jesse Wilcox Smith as a child, and learned to appreciate the beauty there. When I attended art school, I always tried to bring that spirit into my work.

The Children's Beading Book was written for children who love beads and want to work with them. Adults can also use this book; it was written with a slightly different approach that all bead lovers can appreciate.

As a mom, I realize the importance of activities that nurture the creative process. As much as I love television and playing on the internet, when it comes right down to it, you can't beat the wonderful feeling you get when you create. Art is not just in a museum, or something that hangs on a wall in some obscure gallery; it is anything you make with your hands that you create with love. The loveliest of gifts are those that have been handmade.

The projects in this book are suitable for children of many ages. They are easy to master, and work up quickly. They take a minimum investment of money, and yet will keep them happy and busy for hours. However, if a child is prone to putting things in their mouth, they do need to be monitored with small objects like beads. It's not a good idea to hand a bead to a very young child, because it can disappear into their mouths in the wink of an eye!

I hope you enjoy this book. This is part of a series of 25 books called **The Beading Books Series.** Other books in the series include *The Best Little Beading Book, The Beaded Lampshade Book, The Magical Beaded Medicine Bag Book, The "Knotty" Macrame and Beading Book, The Beaded Watchband Book, The Chain & Crystal Book* and *The Beaded Jewelry for a Wedding Book.*

As always, I love hearing your wonderful comments. Please feel free to write to me c/o The Interstellar Trading and Publishing Company, Post Office Box 2215, La Mesa, CA 91943.

Happy Beading!™

"Me"

Table of Contents

Beads and Materials

Why is it when a child wants to make something, everyone hands her macaroni, beans, or some other stringable edible thing, and that's supposed to be enough? If you put the time into making something, it's so much nicer to use real beads.

Beads come from around the world, and the variety is wonderful. There is something for every budget. You can go to the flea market and buy bags of junk jewelry (to take apart and use the beads) for almost no money at all; you can ask relatives for disgarded pieces that you can redesign and restring; or you can buy beads at bead or craft stores. Here are some of the most common you can work with.

Plastic Beads

Usually the least expensive, these come in bright colors with a lot of variety. They usually have larger holes, which makes stringing easier. You have to be careful not to get the really poor quality ones with bad seams, although any bead will do for practice.

Seedbeads

These are the very small beads that are used for weaving projects and more intricate beadwork. They are sized, so it is important to always get the size specified in the patterns. It's a strange system: the higher the number, the smaller the bead. A size 11/0 seedbead is considered the standard; a 10/0 is larger, and a 12/0 is smaller. The Moon and Shooting Star Medicine Bag takes size 6/0 seedbeads, which are a lot larger than 11/0's, and work up very quickly. Remember, if you change the size of the bead you use, it will change the size and appearance of the finished project.

Semi Precious Beads

These are natural stones that have been drilled. There is a large variety of them available. Rose Quartz (pink), Lapis (blue), Turquoise (blue-green), and Amethyst (purple) are some of the most common. Gemshows and beadstores usually have a good selection of these.

Glass Beads

Glass beads have a very nice quality, and the price is reasonable. Look for beads from Czech Republic or India for the best variety.

Other Beads, Buttons, and Charms

When you attend a gem show or go to a bead store, you might feel a little overwhelmed by the variety. Look at crystal beads, handmade glass beads, coral, sea shells, metal beads, polymer clay beads, and wooden beads.

Go through old button boxes for buttons that you can use in your jewelry. These can be strung like beads or used as a clasp.

Charms add something wonderful, too. You might even consider using gum machine toys (I have a box of them from when I was a child. They add a bit of fun to your creations).

Findings

A finding is anything that is not a bead. For example, clasps, metal enhancers, pendants, etc. There is an endless variety, so it's just a matter of deciding which findings you like to work with. The illustrations below show some of what is available.

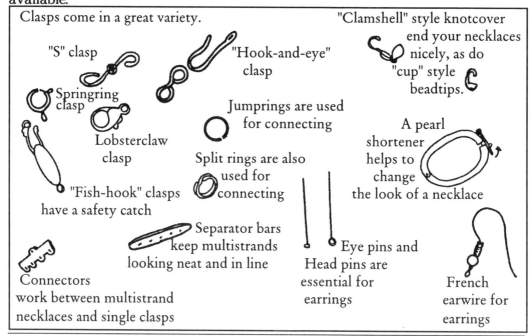

Clasps come in a great variety.

"S" clasp

"Hook-and-eye" clasp

"Clamshell" style knotcover end your necklaces nicely, as do "cup" style beadtips.

Springring clasp

Lobsterclaw clasp

Jumprings are used for connecting

A pearl shortener helps to change the look of a necklace

"Fish-hook" clasps have a safety catch

Split rings are also used for connecting

Connectors work between multistrand necklaces and single clasps

Separator bars keep multistrands looking neat and in line

Eye pins and Head pins are essential for earrings

French earwire for earrings

You really won't need to purchase a lot of tools to make these projects. Depending on the projects you choose, you should only need a few things.

Needles

The most useful is a little twisted wire needle that works great with pearls and other beads. It has a collapsible eye and is very flexible. It fits through most beads easily. However, it's not super-sturdy, and won't last through many necklaces.

The number 10 or 12 English beading needle works best with seedbeads. Be careful, because it it small and sharp!

A dental flossing needle is great for many children. It's not sharp, and has a huge eye that's easy to thread. It's perfect for beads with larger holes; smaller beads don't work with it if their holes are small. You'll find this in the dental supply department at the drug store!

Threads
The easiest stringing materials don't require needles. Tiger Tail and Soft Flex wire are coated wires. They are stiff, and easy to work with. Tiger Tail shouldn't be knotted, Soft Flex is knotable. You usually use "crimp" beads with these, which are small beads that are crushed with a plier. The Glass Bead Necklace and Red and Yellow Necklace are made with this technique.

The most used thread is a silk or nylon bead cord. You can purchase this on a card with a needle already attached, or by the spool. It comes in different weights. "F" (#3) is your general purpose weight that works with most beads. The variety of colors is wonderful.

Nymo is used for working with seedbeads. It's usually white or black, but sometimes it is available in colors, too.

Tools

Pointed tweezers are helpful in making knots.

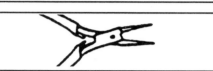

Chain nose pliers are useful for making earrings and working with chain and wire.

A bead loom is one of the most enjoyable tools for beading. You can make many types of projects, and it's always fun and easy to work with.

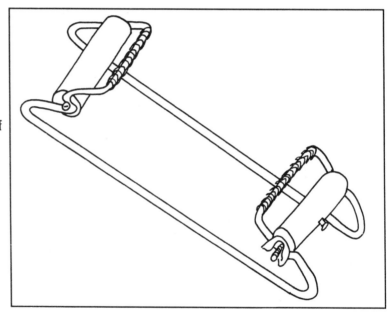

Elizabeth and Ben

"I am soooo bored," Elizabeth sighed loudly as she looked at her brother, Ben. Ben looked up from his book. They were spending the weekend at their aunt's house. It was raining, and there was nothing to do. "We can't play outside, we can't go anywhere," Elizabeth stood at the window, looking at the rain. "This storm will never end," they wailed.

Aunt Matilda didn't like seeing the children so bored. "Why don't the two of you go play in the attic? I'm sure there are plenty of things to keep you both interested"

The children climbed the stairs that led to the attic. It was dark, and smelled damp from the rain. They turned on the lights, and gasped. They had forgotten how filled with treasures the attic was.

There were boxes filled with old clothes; strange unrecognizable things made of wire; old bicycles and bird cages, and lots of odd stuff.

But the most mysterious of all was an old treasure chest in the corner of the room.

Elizabeth and Ben ran to the chest. At first it was very difficult to open, but they worked together until finally the top opened. Never had a treasure chest been filled like this! There were beads and buttons right up to the top. Even though the children had seen beads many times before, they had never seen beads like these! They were every color and size you could imagine.

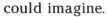

There were beads made of glass, shell, stone, wood, and of crystal. They danced in the light and and sparkled and shined. They were magic!

Eagerly they started digging in the chest. Without hesitation, they looked at each other and said, "We've got to make something!"

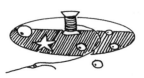

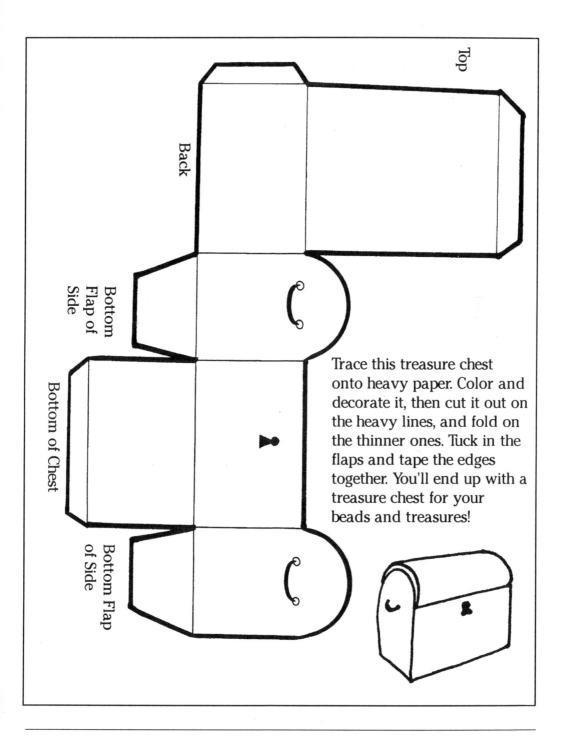

Top

Back

Bottom Flap of Side

Bottom of Chest

Bottom Flap of Side

Trace this treasure chest onto heavy paper. Color and decorate it, then cut it out on the heavy lines, and fold on the thinner ones. Tuck in the flaps and tape the edges together. You'll end up with a treasure chest for your beads and treasures!

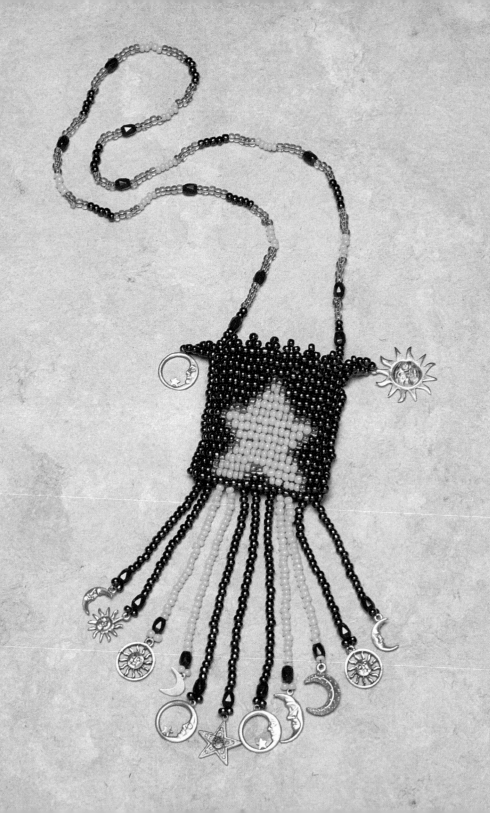

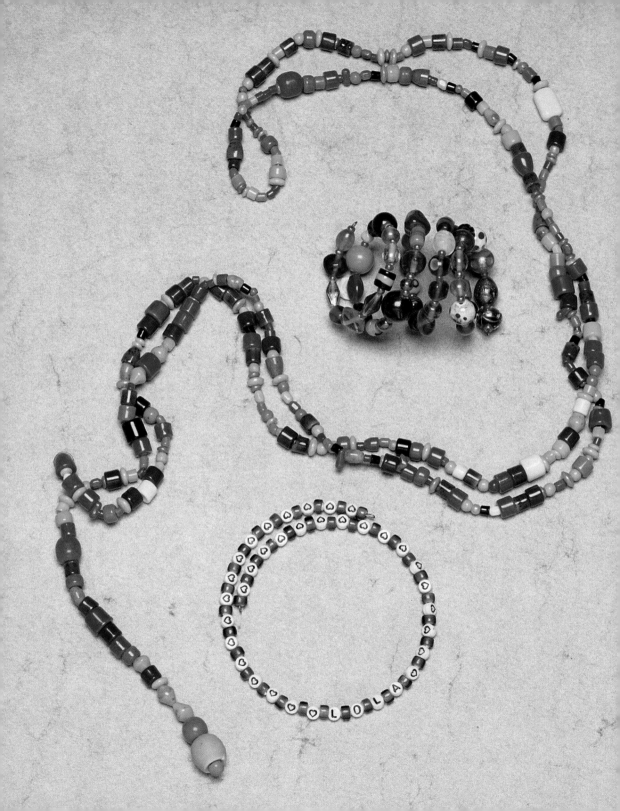

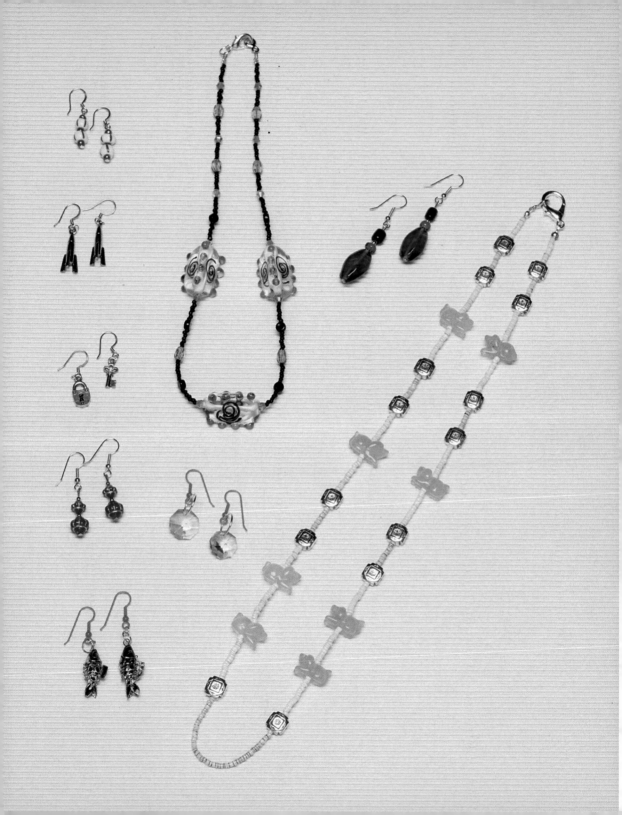

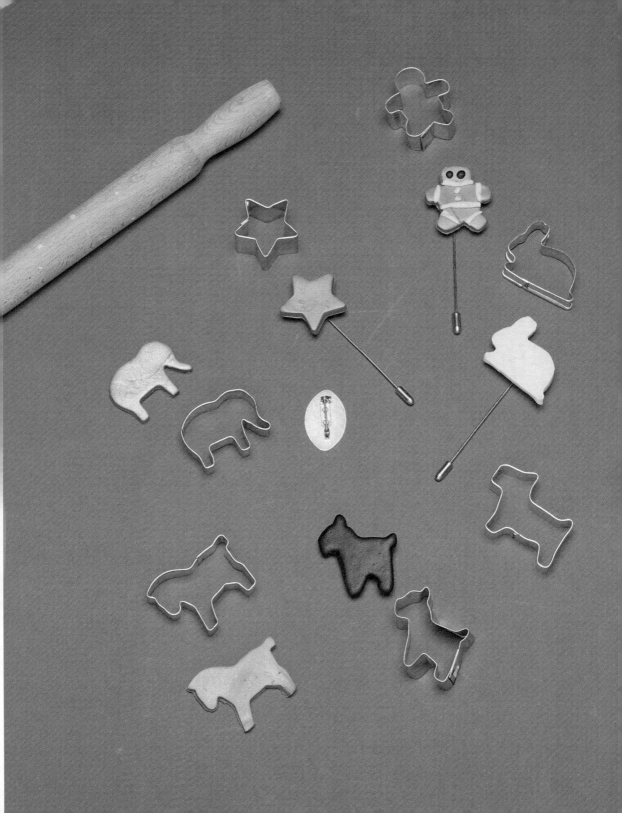

Painting Beads

Elizabeth and Ben found large wooden beads and marking pens. The beads were very plain, and not decorated at all. The two children started drawing on them, and soon they had very beautiful beads.

SUPPLIES NEEDED:

Wooden beads
Permanent marking pens in assorted colors
Optional: white vinegar and spray fixative

STEP ONE:

Clean your wooden beads with white vinegar before you start.

Let them dry completely.

STEP TWO:

Plan your designs in pencil first. Fill in the colors before you outline in marker, so it won't smear.

STEP THREE:

Outline in black to give your design definition.

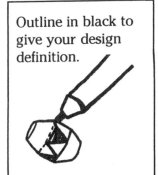

STEP FOUR:

Let them completely dry. If possible, spray lightly with a fixative to protect the color.

You can make all types of designs on your beads!

A Cord or Leather Necklace

Now that you have all of these beautiful beads that you made yourself, you can string them onto a fun necklace.

There are many types of cording or leather strands that you can use.

- RAT TAIL is shiny satin cording that comes in a lot of colors.
- LEATHER CORDING comes in black, brown, tan, or sometimes its dipped to make other colors.
- SOUTACHE is a braided cord that looks very fancy.

SUPPLIES NEEDED:

Your decorated beads
One yard of cording

STEP ONE:

String your beads onto the leather.

STEP TWO:

Center them, and make an overhand knot on either side of the beads.

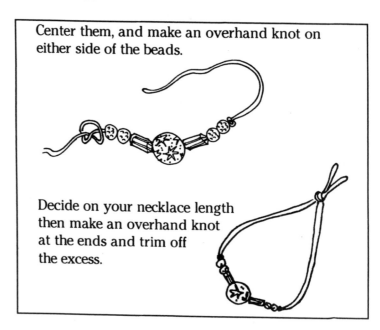

Decide on your necklace length then make an overhand knot at the ends and trim off the excess.

Penguin Key Ring

Elizabeth and Ben knew that Aunt Matilda was always misplacing her keys. So they made her this keyring with the beads that they decorated mixed with other beads from the chest.

MATERIALS:

- Leather cording
- One wooden bead designed to look like a penguin (or whatever you like)
- One other large wooden decorated bead
- An assortment of pony beads
- One split ring made for keys

STEP ONE:

Start by making a folding your leather in half and making a halfhitch knot to anchor it to the keyring.

STEP TWO:

Make an overhand knot right after the half hitch knot, then start adding beads to the leather.

STEP THREE:

Finish with an overhand knot to keep your beads in place. Trim the extra leather away from the ends.

The Children's Beading Book

Polymer Clay Pins

Elizabeth and Ben decided it was time to take a break. They went downstairs to the kitchen. Aunt Matilda was baking cookies. The children watched her roll out the dough, then cut it into shapes with cookie cutters.

Working with polymer clay is just like making cookies. The big difference, of course, is that you cannot eat polymer clay. You can use the same types of tools as if you were baking, but once you've used them for the clay, you shouldn't use them on food again. Elizabeth and Ben found an old toy baking set from when they were little. It had a rolling pin and toy cookie cutters in it. This worked out perfectly for what they wanted to make..

The children took turns softening the clay - sometimes it needs a little help before it's ready to work with. They squeezed it and oozed it through their fingers, until it felt soft and would roll out without cracking. They got wax paper from Aunt Matilda, and rolled out the clay on it until it was about 1/8 inch thick. Then, they got really creative!

MATERIALS:

- Polymer clay
- A rolling pin, plastic knife, and cookie cutters
- Jewelry findings (pin backs, earring findings, etc.)
- Cement
- Wax paper

STEP ONE:

Roll out your clay. Use your cookie cutters to make shapes.
Decorate with beads, other clay, etc.

STEP TWO:

Bake the clay according to package directions. Let cool completely. Carefully cement your findings onto the back of each piece.

STEP THREE:

You now have beautiful pins and earrings to give as gifts, or wear yourself!

Working With Memory Wire

As Elizabeth and Ben started up the stairs to the attic, they spied a coil of wire. Aunt Matilda told them it was "memory wire." It is called that because it always keeps its shape: no matter how many beads you add to it, it will always be in a coil. And, it fits everybody, because you adjust the size by how tightly you wind it onto someone's wrist. Elizabeth and Ben decided to make Aunt Matilda a bracelet, to thank her for the wonderful cookies.

To make a simple coiled bracelet:

MATERIALS NEEDED:
- A length of memory wire five coils
    long
- Enough beads to fill (appx. 16") wire
- One head pin (optional)
- Your pliers

By the time you add your beads, this bracelet will only be about 3 coils
    long.

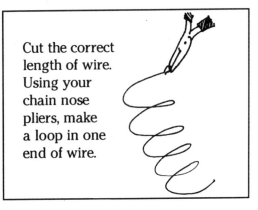

Cut the correct length of wire. Using your chain nose pliers, make a loop in one end of wire.

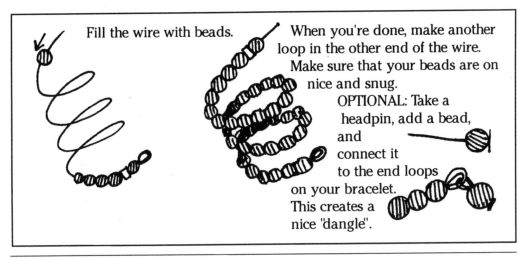

Fill the wire with beads.

When you're done, make another loop in the other end of the wire. Make sure that your beads are on nice and snug.

OPTIONAL: Take a headpin, add a bead, and connect it to the end loops on your bracelet. This creates a nice "dangle".

Memory Wire Chokers

Elizabeth and Ben decided to make a necklace for their friend Lola, using memory wire made for necklaces. They found it was very easy to make a single strand memory wire choker.

MATERIALS NEEDED:
- A length of memory wire long enough to go around the neck once
- Thirty seven 5mm pony beads (they used lavender)
- Thirty-two "letter" beads with hearts on them*
- The letters of their friend's name : L - O - L - A *

*There are 36 letter beads needed. You will probably have to adjust the number of hearts and letters for the name of the person you are making this for.
- Your pliers and wire cutters

Just as you did with the bracelet, make a loop in the beginning of the wire, add your beads and make a loop at the finishing end of the wire to secure.

It doesn't need a clasp, because it holds its shape.

Memory wire is also available for rings.

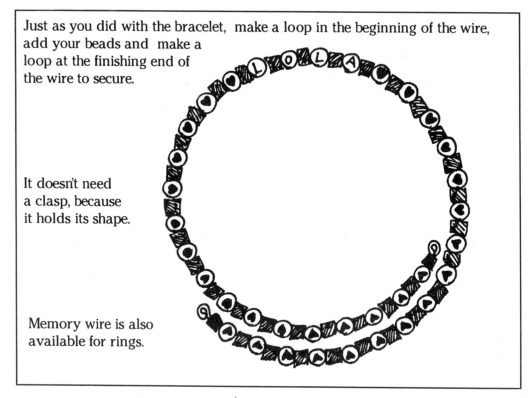

It's nice to have earrings to match the necklaces you make. This style of earring is easy, and doesn't take that many materials. You can use eye pins (with loops) or head pins (with a flat head). You'll want two of everything (for two earrings). You'll need head or eye pins, two of every bead, and earwires.

STEP ONE:

Thread your beads on a pin in the desired order.

STEP TWO:

Cut the pin with wirecutters 1/2 inch from the top of the last bead.

STEP THREE:

Bend the top of the pin at an angle with your pliers.

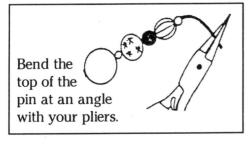

STEP FOUR:

Thread the earwire on the pin.

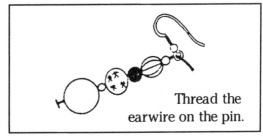

STEP THREE:

With your pliers, bend the pin to make a nice, smooth loop.

STEP FOUR:

Finish by making sure that the loop is closed nice and tight.

A great gift!

Using Jumprings

Jumprings are easy to work with, and you can do so many things with them! If you have charms or gum machine toys, you can use jumprings to incorporate them into your jewelry.

HOW TO WORK WITH JUMPRINGS:

Jumprings are sometimes called "O" rings. They are used for joining two items that have holes in them together. The thing to remember about them is that you have to be careful when you open them, or you will ruin their shape. Always twist them sideways when you are opening them, because if you pull them apart to open them, they will be pulled out of shape, and it's almost impossible to get the curve right again. After you have opened the ring, add your charm and your earwire, then carefully swivel the ring sideways to close. Be sure that you have closed the ring tightly, so that nothing comes apart. It helps to work with two pliers.

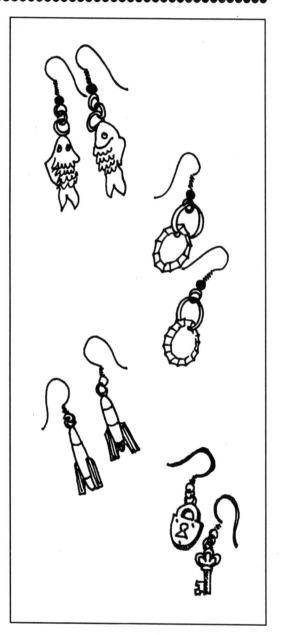

The Children's Beading Book

Lucky Charms

You can make many things using charms. They make great holiday gifts. Try using bats and spiders for Halloween earrings; shamrocks for St. Patricks Day; or sports charms to cheer on your favorite team. Charms are available in bead and craft stores. Sometimes you can use an old charm bracelet for great variety.

Crystal Fairy Necklace

Using the techniques for jumprings and head pins, you can make this beautiful necklace. Use head pins with the crystal beads, and jumprings with the fairy charms. Use a chain that has large links, so it will be easy to work with. Use as many charms and beads as you like.

The Children's Beading Book

Beaded Belt

Making a beaded belt is a great way to dress up a simple outfit.

MATERIALS NEEDED:
- one bag of mixed beads
- nylon bead cord in size 4 or FF
- one dental flossing needle
- cement

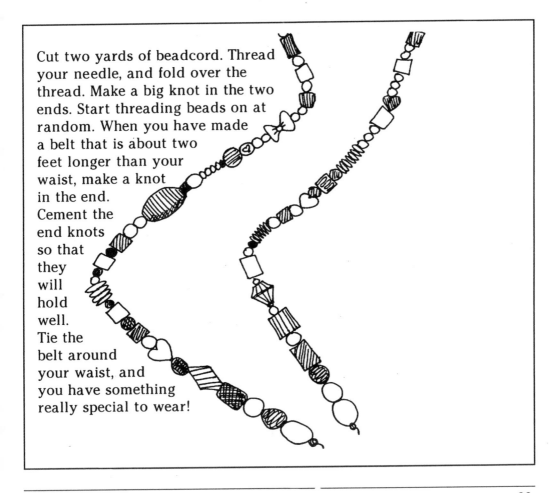

Cut two yards of beadcord. Thread your needle, and fold over the thread. Make a big knot in the two ends. Start threading beads on at random. When you have made a belt that is about two feet longer than your waist, make a knot in the end. Cement the end knots so that they will hold well. Tie the belt around your waist, and you have something really special to wear!

Tigertail and Softflex wire are two cables used for stringing. The reason that they're called a cable, and not a thread, is because they are nylon-coated wires. They are stronger than thread, and are worked with a little differently.

Softflex wire can be knotted. It is stiffer than regular thread and comes in a lot of beautiful colors. You can also use crimp beads with it, which is a more traditional method of working with wires. Tigertail cannot be knotted; it will kink up.

Crimp beads are tiny little gold or silvertone beads that are used to end the necklace. You use two per side, near the clasp, and then you crush them with a plier. That's because there are little teeth inside each bead, and when you've crushed them good and tight, the little teeth imbed themselves into the nylon coating on the wire, and it holds the necklace together.

You can use tiger tail for necklaces, bracelets, and it's perfect for anklets, too.

HOW TO WORK WITH COATED STRINGING WIRES:

STEP ONE:

Cut a length of tigertail or Softflex wire 12 inches longer thatn your intended necklace length. Adhere a piece of scotch tape to one end.

STEP TWO:

String your beads onto the wire. If you change your mind or make a mistake, simply remove the tape and make the change, without having to restring everything.

STEP THREE:

Add 2 crimp beads, your clasp, and return the wire back through the crimp beads. Make sure that you leave enough wire to complete the second side.

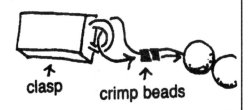

clasp   **crimp beads**

STEP FOUR:

With a plier, crush the crimp beads. Be careful that they're where you want them to be, and that your clasp hasn't wandered into the grip of the pliers (it will get c
If possible, fe
tigertail bacl
through
some of
the beads.

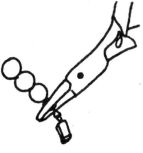

STEP FIVE:

Let the strand hang vertically (clasp open) to help remove kinks from the tiger tail. Carefully run your hand down the strand to smooth out any remaining kinks.

STEP SIX:

Repeat like the first side. (2 crimps, the clasp, and back through the crimps, adjusting the tension. Now, crimp carefully.

Trim away the excess wire that you were able to feed back through the beads.

trim

Glass Bead Necklace

Using the same techniques described in the two previous pages, you can make this glass bead necklace.

MATERIALS NEEDED:

- Three large fancy glass beads
- Six aqua colored 10 x 7 mm Czech crystal
- Twelve 4mm green Czech crystal
- Six black 5mm round glass beads
- 154 black size 10/0 seedbeads
- Four crimp beads
- One clasp
- 30 inches of light blue Softflex wire

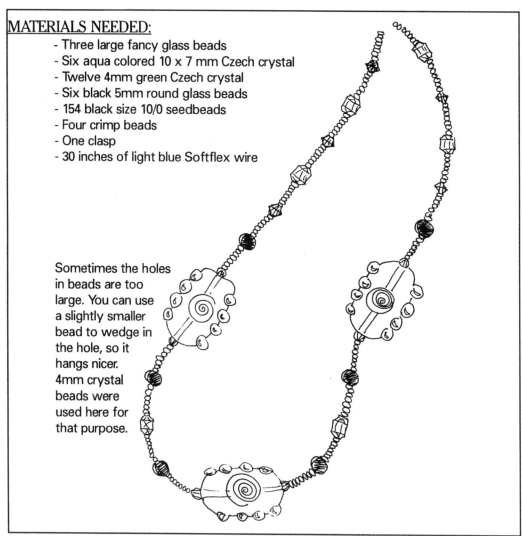

Sometimes the holes in beads are too large. You can use a slightly smaller bead to wedge in the hole, so it hangs nicer. 4mm crystal beads were used here for that purpose.

Red and Yellow Earring and Necklace Set

Elizabeth and Ben found these beads in the bottom of the old chest. They are very unusual, and brightly colored. They are handmade glass beads. They decided to make an earring and necklace set for the nice woman next door.

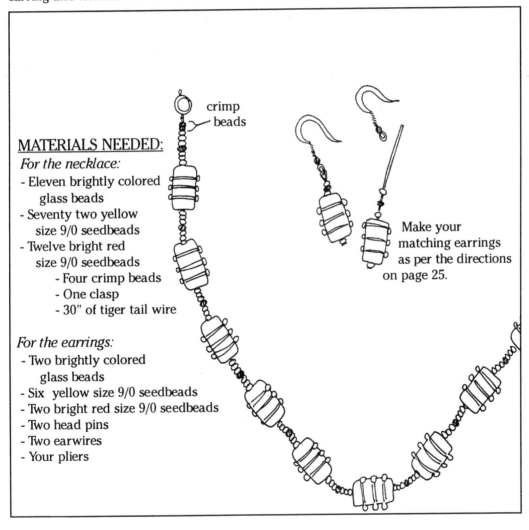

crimp beads

MATERIALS NEEDED:

For the necklace:
- Eleven brightly colored glass beads
- Seventy two yellow size 9/0 seedbeads
- Twelve bright red size 9/0 seedbeads
    - Four crimp beads
    - One clasp
    - 30" of tiger tail wire

For the earrings:
- Two brightly colored glass beads
- Six yellow size 9/0 seedbeads
- Two bright red size 9/0 seedbeads
- Two head pins
- Two earwires
- Your pliers

Make your matching earrings as per the directions on page 25.

Basic Necklace Stringing

Besides tigertail and Softflex wire, many people like to use silk or nylon bead cord for their beads. This is easy to knot. You can use knot covers to give your necklace a nicer look, and it will last longer.

WORKING WITH KNOT COVERS:

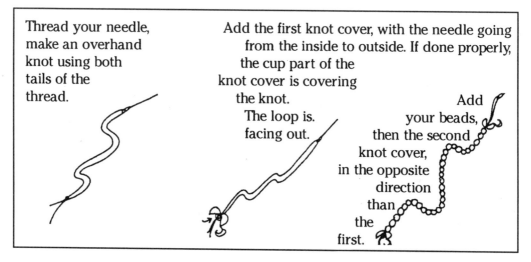

Thread your needle, make an overhand knot using both tails of the thread.

Add the first knot cover, with the needle going from the inside to outside. If done properly, the cup part of the knot cover is covering the knot. The loop is. facing out.

Add your beads, then the second knot cover, in the opposite direction than the first.

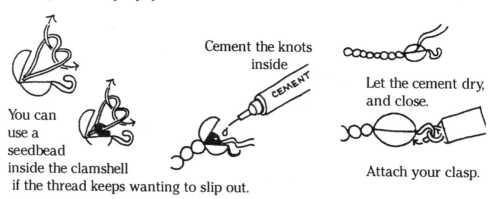

Make a couple of square knots tightly in the clamshell of the knot cover (or in the cup of the cup style).

You can use a seedbead inside the clamshell if the thread keeps wanting to slip out.

Cement the knots inside

Let the cement dry, and close.

Attach your clasp.

Rose Quartz Puppy Necklace

Rose Quartz is a pretty pink natural stone. Sometimes you can find it in fun shapes. Elizabeth and Ben found rose quartz puppies, and they mixed them with silver Southwest looking beads and shell heishi beads to make a fun Southwest necklace.

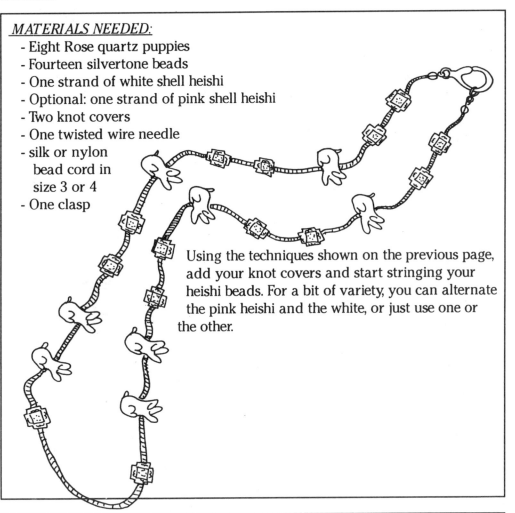

MATERIALS NEEDED:
- Eight Rose quartz puppies
- Fourteen silvertone beads
- One strand of white shell heishi
- Optional: one strand of pink shell heishi
- Two knot covers
- One twisted wire needle
- silk or nylon bead cord in size 3 or 4
- One clasp

Using the techniques shown on the previous page, add your knot covers and start stringing your heishi beads. For a bit of variety, you can alternate the pink heishi and the white, or just use one or the other.

Ben likes to work with word games. He got so excited with all of the beads and the jewelry that they were making, that he decided to make up a crossword puzzle.

CLUES:

ACROSS:

1. What you wear on your finger
4. You put the thread through this on a bead
6. This goes around your neck
8. Every necklace has a beginning and an _____ .
10. Elizabeth and Ben did this to the cookies that Aunt Matilda baked:
    They liked to _____ them.
11. You use this with a thread
12. A type of beadwork that makes a strong netting of beads
    (Hint: you use a loom)

DOWN:

1. Most beads are this shape
2. You use this with a needle
3. This goes on your wrist
5. You use this to weave beads
7. A type of bead that sparkles and shines
9. What Elizabeth and Ben found lots of in the treasure chest: _____ s

Answers are on page 50

	16/0
	15/0
	14/0
	13/0
	12/0
	11/0
	10/0
	9/0
	8/0
	7/0
	6/0
	5/0
	4/0
	3/0
	2/0
	1/0

Seedbeads are wonderful to work with. They are smaller, and do require more patience, but they your hard work will be rewarded with beautiful, intricate patterns and delicate designs that larger beads just can't compete with.

As previously mentioned, seedbeads come in different sizes. The larger the number, the smaller the bead; the smaller the number, the larger the bead.

This chart on the left shows the differences in sizes. It's not a good idea to substitute different sizes than those called for in a pattern. Whenever possible, always use exactly what the pattern calls for.

Size 11/0 is the most common. People like it because it is easy to work with, and a convenient size.

Seedbeads also have different finishes. They can be shiny, dull, transparent, or opaque.

Some are really shiny, and have a silver lining. These are called Rocailles. They come in a lot of colors, and look nice for fancier projects.

Opaque seedbeads, also called Indian beads, are a very nice, even shape, and work well for the beadloom.

Iris seedbeads have a glossy, translucent appearance; Lustre seedbeads have a bright, glossy look; Metallic seedbeads look like metal.

Most seedbeads are made out of glass.

Whichever ones you choose, they will always look great.

Seedbead and Wire Rings

This is a great way to use odds and ends of seedbeads to make nice rings. You can even add crystal if you like, to make a fancy "stone".

MATERIALS NEEDED:

- 28 gauge wire
- An assortment of seedbeads and crystals (optional)
- Wire cutters

Cut a one foot length of wire.
Thread on three seedbeads.

Center the beads on the wrie. Bend up the sides, and add 3 more seedbeads. Crisscross your wire through the seedbeads.

Keep working like so, adding beads and crisscrossing wire through them. If you want a ring that widens at the top, experiment with different effects by adding beads two at a time. When you have the right length then you are done. Weave the ends together being sure not to leave any exposed wire, and trim.

Bent Wire Rings

While you're making rings, you might want to try this one. It's really easy, and you can use all sorts of beads.

MATERIALS NEEDED:

- 18 gauge wire and 24 gauge wire
- An assortment of beads
- Two pliers
- Wire cutters
- A wooden dowel, about 3/4 inch
  in diameter

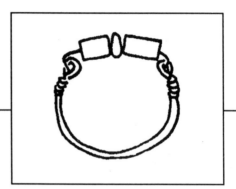

Cut a 2" piece of 18 gauge wire and wrap it loosely around your dowel. This makes a nice curve for your ring. Now, readjust for sizing

Using your pliers, bend the wire to form a small loop at one end. Cut the wire to fit 3/4 of the way around your finger, then bend the second end in a small loop.

Be sure that the loops are parallel to each other.

Thread beads on a length of 24 gauge wire. Wrap the end smoothly through the loop of the 18 gauge, and coil carefully.

Thread the other end of the wrie through the other loop of the 18 gauge, and coil tightly to match the other side.

Here's a guide for your ring size. Trace it, and cut it out. Then, try it on for size!

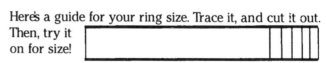

5 6 7 89 10

Seedbead Daisy Chain Necklace

Elizabeth and Ben wanted to make something a little different. They had lots of seedbeads to work with, but didn't know what to make. So, they went downstairs to Aunt Matilda, and she showed them how to make this pretty daisy chain necklace.

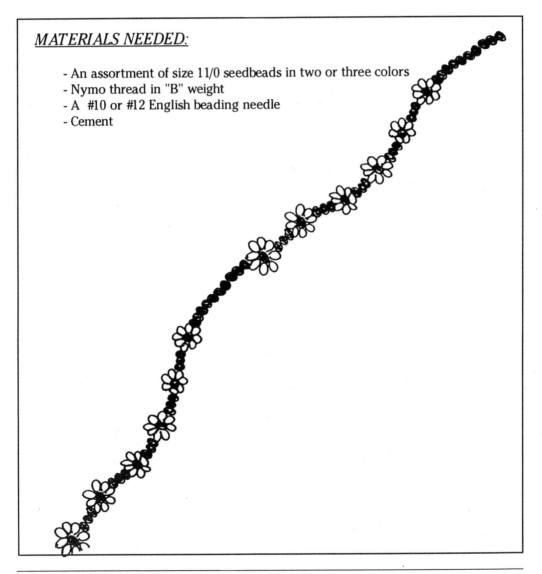

MATERIALS NEEDED:

- An assortment of size 11/0 seedbeads in two or three colors
- Nymo thread in "B" weight
- A #10 or #12 English beading needle
- Cement

STEP ONE:

Cut a length of nymo about 3" long. Thread your needle. Make a little knot about 2" from the end. Add 3 beads in Color A, Then 4 beads in Color B, Then 1 bead in Color C.

STEP TWO:

After going through the beads described in Step One, go back through the last 3 beads in Color B.

STEP THREE:

Go back through these 3 Color B, Color C, then add 4 more beads in Color B.

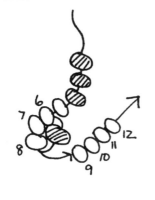

STEP FOUR:

Bring your needle through that first Color B bead.

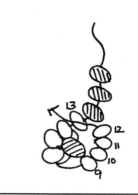

STEP FIVE:

Bring your needle through Color C, then back through bead number 9.

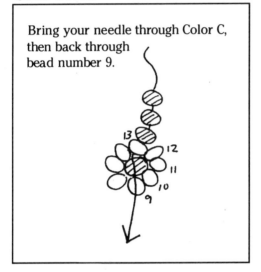

STEP SIX:

Add 3 more beads in Color A

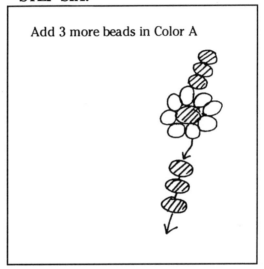

STEP SEVEN:

Add 4 beads in Color B.

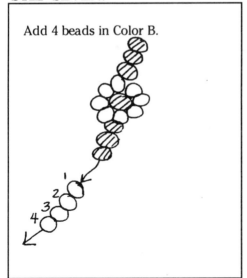

STEP EIGHT:

The whole process starts all over.

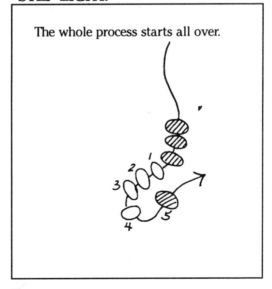

Using a beading loom takes a lot of concentration, but it creates a very beautiful project.

PARTS OF A BEADLOOM

The most common beadloom is the wire variety that you find in most craft stores. It consists of a wire frame, two wooden dowels, and a springlike-part that keeps your threads separate

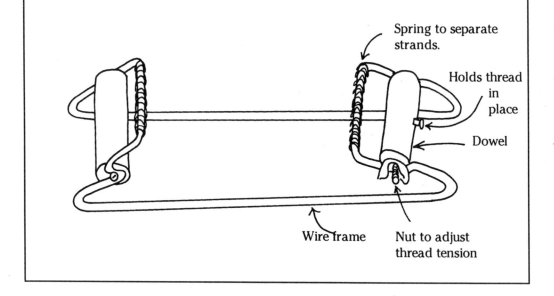

Spring to separate strands.

Holds thread in place

Dowel

Wire frame

Nut to adjust thread tension

The easiest way to thread a loom is to cut a lot of threads the same length, and make a knot in one end. Remember, when deciding how many threads you need, you will have one more thread than the number of beads in the width of your design. So, if your pattern is 20 beads wide, you will use 21 threads.

Secure the threads on one of the little nails attached to the dowels. Pull tightly as you stretch the thread across.

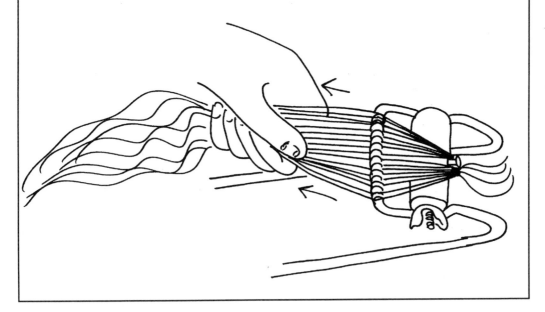

Pull the threads tightly across, and secure on the second dowel. Your threads should lay nice and parallel, like the strings on a guitar.

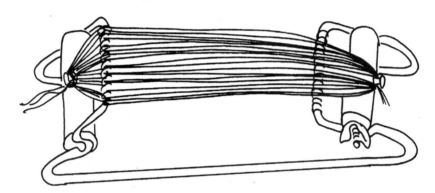

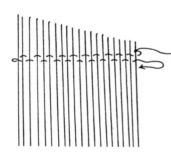

Thread your number 10 or 12 English beading needle, and tie a knot in the end that attaches it to the righthand most thread. Start weaving in and out (like lawnchair webbing) to strengthen the ends. Do this for several rows.

When you add your rows of be the objective is to have one bea in each open area between strands.

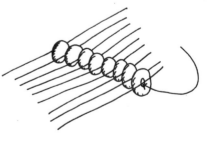

The secret to the beads being locked on the loom and not coming off is that the thread passes through each row of beads twice. The first time, you line up the beads with each open area, and the thread passes under the strands already on the loom. You then bring your needle in a U-turn through the same row of beads, but this time, it is passing on top of the strands in the loom. So, it is locked into place.

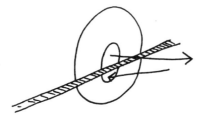

Use your finger to push the beads up as you work. This will help them stay in alignment.

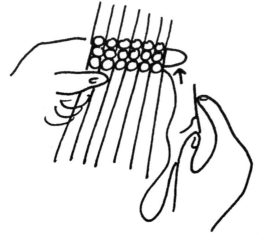

Moon and Shooting Star Medicine Bag

To make this bag, you'll use the techniques for looming from the previous pages. The pattern is actually for the whole bag, so one side is right side up, and the other is upside down. Work the whole pattern, then it will be folded in half when you are done.

This is a more advanced project. You may want to practice on the loom first until you feel comfortable with the technique.

MATERIALS NEEDED:
- Irridenscent blue size 9/0 seedbeads
- Transparent lavender size 9/0 seedbeads
- Yellow size 9/0 seedbeads
- One bead loom
- Miscellaneous charms
- Miscellaneous crystal beads
- One beadloom
- Nymo, size "B"
- English beading needles, Size 10 or 12 (you may need more than one if they break)

Start by threading 21 strands on the loom. Work the pattern shown on page 50. Carefully take the bag off of the loom, and weave the ends in so that there are no loose threads.

FINISHING THE MEDICINE BAG

When you have finished weaving in your loose ends, fol
the bag over.

Stitch up the sides, adding a bead to cover your stitches.

To make the picot stitching
on the top, Add three beads,
skip one bead, go through
the next bead, and so on,
across the top of the bag.

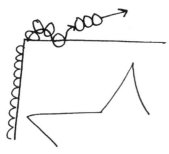

To make your fringe, line them up with the
rows of beads. Go down through the beads,
add a charm to the end, back up through the
fringe, secure by going through a bead, and
move onto the next one.

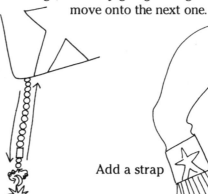

Add a strap

Add loops at the side for the two last charms.

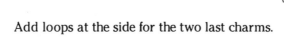

Congratulations! This does take a lot
of patience!

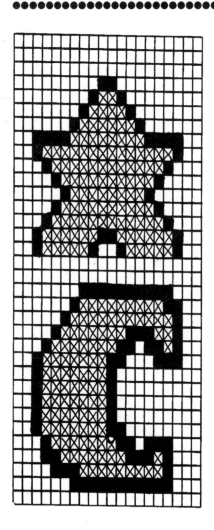

Here are the answers to Ben's crossword puzzle:

ACROSS:
1. Ring
4. Hole
6. Necklace
8. End
10. Eat
11. Needle
12. Weave

DOWN:
1. Round
2. Thread
3. Bracelet
5. Loom
7. Crystal
9. Bead

Wendy Simpson Conner is no stranger to beads. As a third-generation bead artist, she grew up with beads from a very early age. Her grandmother was the jewelry and costume designer for the Ziegfeld Follies.

Being from a creative family, Wendy spent her childhood doing many types of crafts in a rural community. ("There just wasn't anything else to do!"). Over the years, she has mastered many techniques, but beads have remained her first love.

She worked as a designer in television for awhile, and also has a strong illustration background (she always insists on doing her own illustrations).

Wendy has been teaching vocational beadwork classes for San Diego Community Colleges and the Grossmont Adult School District for fifteen years. She not only teaches beading technique, but also the dynamics of running your own jewelry business.

Her first book, *The Best Little Beading Book,* was the result of many of her classroom handouts. All of her books, including *The Beaded Lampshade Book, The Magical Beaded Medicine Bag Book, The "Knotty" Macrame and Beading Book, The Beaded Watchband Book , The Chain & Crystal Book,* and *The Beaded Jewelry for a Wedding Book,* have been very popular. They are part of **The Beading Books Series,** a collection of 25 books devoted to preserving beading techniques and history.

Wendy designs jewelry for several television shows, as well as the celebrities on them.

Recently, she produced, wrote and directed *The Bead Movement,* the critically acclaimed documentary which examines the world's fascination with beads.

Wendy is available to teach workshops. If you are interested, please contact her through the Interstellar Publishing Company, Post Office Box 2215, La Mesa, California, 91943.

INTERSTELLAR

TRADING & PUBLISHING COMPANY

Other Books By the

Interstellar Trading & Publishing Company:

☀ *The Best Little Beading Book* ☀

☀ *The Beaded Lampshade Book* ☀

☀ *The Magical Beaded Medicine Bag Book*

☀ *The "Knotty" Macrame & Beading Book* ☀

☀ *The Beaded Watchband Book* ☀

☀ *The Chain & Crystal Book* ☀

☀ *The Beaded Jewelry for a Wedding Book* ☀

☀ *The Children's Beading Book* ☀

☀ *The Cat Lover's Beaded Project Book* ☀

If you would like a list of other titles and forthcoming books from the Interstellar Trading & Publishing Company, please send a stamped, self-addressed envelope to:

THE INTERSTELLAR TRADING & PUBLISHING COMPANY
POST OFFICE BOX 2215
LA MESA, CALIFORNIA, 91943